This SUPER
annual belongs
to a HERO called

. . . .

Write your name here

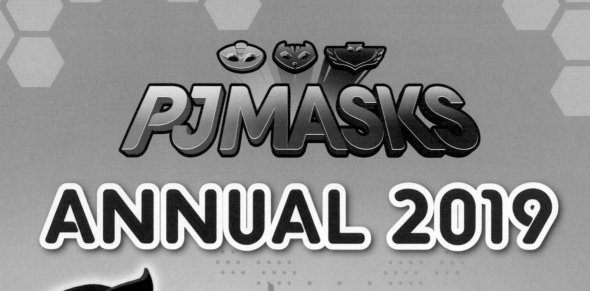

ANNUAL 2019

pat a Cake

CONTENTS

HERE COME THE PJ MASKS

Who are the heroes inside the PJ Masks' incredible super suits? Meet Amaya, Connor and Greg.

WE MIGHT LOOK LIKE ORDINARY KIDS . . .

AND THESE MIGHT LOOK LIKE ORDINARY PYJAMAS . . .

BUT WHEN DARKNESS FALLS, EVERYTHING CHANGES.

AMAYA

GREG

CONNOR

ARE YOU READY FOR AN ADVENTURE? FLIP THE PAGE AS FAST AS YOU CAN!

NIGHT IN THE CITY

A brave band of heroes is ready to face fiendish villains to stop them messing with your day.

AMAYA BECOMES OWLETTE!

CONNOR BECOMES CATBOY!

PJ MASKS, WE'RE ON OUR WAY!   INTO THE NIGHT

HERO HQ

What sort of HQ do the PJ Masks have? Ask a grown-up to help you write the name of each object, then write down the letters in the purple squares in order at the bottom – code cracked!

R [ ] [ ] K

C [ ] [ ] [ ] I [ ]

[ ] K [ ] [ ] B [ ] [ ] [ ] [ ]

T R [ ] [ ]

[ ] O [ ] I [ ]

[ ] E [ ] [ ] [ ] [ ] [ ] [ ] R

T [ ] [ ] [ ] Y

[ ] O [ ] B [ ] [ ] [ ]

C [ ] K [ ]

THE PJ MASKS' HQ IS A

_ _ _ _ _ _ _ _

9

CATBOY DATA

There's only one Catboy – he's brave, bold and can cover huge distances in the blink of an eye! Check out this hero's facts and stats . . .

AWESOME AGILITY

LEADER OF THE PJ MASKS

ASTONISHING EARS

Can hear super-small sounds

NIMBLE AND QUICK

SUPER CAT SPEED

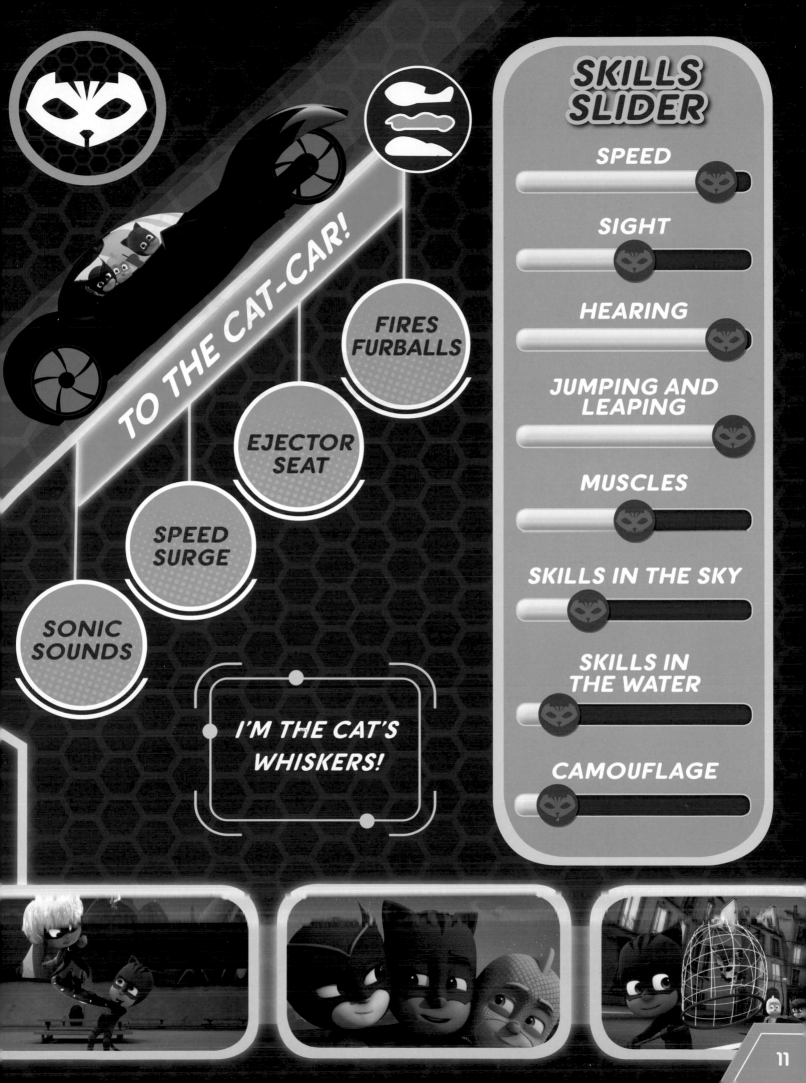

TO THE CAT-CAR!

FIRES FURBALLS

EJECTOR SEAT

SPEED SURGE

SONIC SOUNDS

I'M THE CAT'S WHISKERS!

SKILLS SLIDER

SPEED

SIGHT

HEARING

JUMPING AND LEAPING

MUSCLES

SKILLS IN THE SKY

SKILLS IN THE WATER

CAMOUFLAGE

Catboy is the speediest hero in the city!
How fast can you go? Take this challenge to find out!

YOU WILL NEED: A space that is big enough to run around, either inside or outside.

What To Do:

Make a square using coats, sticks, or anything else you can find to mark the corners. Each side should be at least 15 strides long.

CHOOSE ONE CORNER TO BE THE START.

1
RUN forwards to the next corner and STOP.

2
SIDESTEP to the next corner and STOP.

3
HOP towards the next corner and STOP.

4
RUN forwards to where you started.

Before you start make sure the ground is clear of trip hazards. Catboy always stays on his feet!

You could try:

★ Turning round and going the other way.

★ Doing it all walking backwards, or sidestepping all the way.

★ Making the square larger!

Ask a grown-up or friend to time you. How quickly can you complete the course?

CATBOY

Catboy is great at leaping and jumping. Try this funny game to test your own cat skills!

ISLAND HOP

HOW TO PLAY:

1 Stand still with your feet together.

2 Ask a grown-up to make a square shape, or island, on the floor around you using four strips of sticky tape.

3 Take a BIG Catboy stride, and make another island.

4 Take more strides, left or right, forwards or backwards. When you have five or six islands, the fun can begin!

5 Start in the first square, and JUMP with your feet together into the next one. Now jump again, until you have visited all the islands!

Stay SUPER safe . . . If you don't have room to play inside without bumping into things, play this game outside instead.

YOU WILL NEED:
★ STICKY TAPE
★ A GROWN-UP TO HELP

The PJ Masks' first stop is always their headquarters! By day, it is disguised as a totem pole in the park, but the heroes know that it's so much more.

OWLETTE!

CATBOY!

Grab your favourite pens or pencils, and colour in this cool PJ picture.

ROMEO DATA

Romeo doesn't need any super-powers – he's a baddie with brains! He spends his nights hatching pesky plots and building grim gadgets.

HAS A ROBOT HELPER

WANTS TO RULE THE WORLD!

MARVEL OF MECHANICAL MISCHIEF

CRAZY INVENTOR

MEGA-SMART

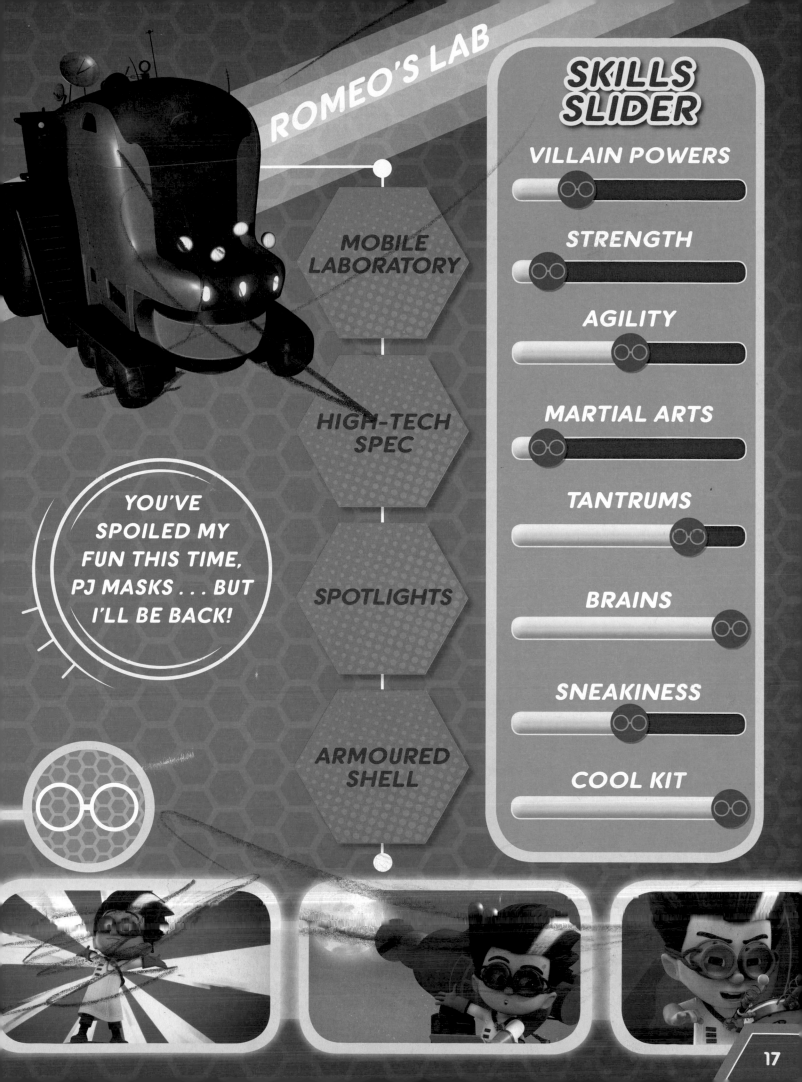

ROMEO'S LAB

SKILLS SLIDER

MOBILE LABORATORY

HIGH-TECH SPEC

SPOTLIGHTS

ARMOURED SHELL

YOU'VE SPOILED MY FUN THIS TIME, PJ MASKS . . . BUT I'LL BE BACK!

VILLAIN POWERS

STRENGTH

AGILITY

MARTIAL ARTS

TANTRUMS

BRAINS

SNEAKINESS

COOL KIT

BOOTCAMP TIME!

Romeo has to keep his brain in tip-top condition if he is going to defeat the PJ Masks! Can you pit your wits against his?

What To Do:

START COUNTING TO 50. SOUNDS EASY? SURE! EXCEPT . . .

Every time you get to a number that includes a 0, shout 'ROMEO RULES'.

Every time you get to a number that includes a 5, make an evil cackling sound.

Every time you get to a number that ends with a 7, strike a villain pose.

Play alone or with a friend to keep your brain as sharp as mine!

Challenging younger or older brainiacs to Romeo's bootcamp blitz?

Change the rules so that everyone can play:

 Younger brainiacs can count up to 10.

Older brainiacs can try counting all the way up to 100.

ROMEO

★ ★ ★

CRAZY CRAYONS

Romeo has set up this super-clever trick. Crack it first, then impress everyone with your brilliant brain!

HOW TO PLAY:

1 Find ten crayons. Choose any colours you like.

2 Carefully lay the crayons out so they match the pattern in the box.

3 Now comes the hard part. Can you take away **TWO** crayons so that you are left with two squares?

If you are stumped, try taking different ones away and putting them back until you find the right answer.

Challenge a friend to solve the crazy crayons. Before you give them the answer, close your eyes and pretend you are thinking REALLY hard!

BADGE OF HONOUR

Each of the PJ Masks has a special badge! Can you spot the badges on their super suits?

If you were a PJ Mask, what would your badge look like? Find some crayons or pencils, then draw it here.

Good work! Now colour in your badge.

TEAM PJ!

Things don't always go to plan, even for the PJ Masks. Catboy, Gekko and Owlette help each other learn from their mistakes. The heroes know that they are stronger together!

Take a look at the team's favourite mottos, then add one of your own. Use the PJ word list to help you.

BELIEVE IN YOURSELF, AND EVERYONE ELSE WILL TOO.

IT'S OKAY TO BE NERVOUS. IT MEANS YOU'RE ABOUT TO DO SOMETHING BRAVE.

MISTAKES ARE PROOF THAT YOU ARE TRYING HARD.

IF SOMETHING DIDN'T QUITE WORK OUT TODAY, THERE IS ALWAYS TOMORROW!

BE AWESOME TODAY!

TOGETHER WE CAN ACHIEVE SO MUCH MORE!

PJ WORD LIST

- kind
- amazing
- loyal
- helpful
- brave
- friendly
- heroic
- incredible

WRITE YOUR OWN MOTTO HERE

....

....

Clumsy Catboy

Connor struggles into class, carrying a model volcano.
"Watch out!" shouts Greg, as it almost smashes onto the floor.
"Connor's being really clumsy today," says Amaya.

"He's not the only one," replies Greg.
Suddenly two of their classmates bump heads and another project rolls off the table.

"No one is usually this clumsy," frowns Amaya. "What's going on?"
This sounds like a job for the PJ Masks . . .

Night falls in the city. The PJ Masks leap into the Cat-Car. The vehicle zigzags through the quiet streets, narrowly missing rubbish bins and lampposts. Catboy is just as clumsy in the night as Connor was in the day!

In the dark, something large lumbers past the heroes.
"Romeo's Lab!" shouts Gekko.

As the Cat-Car lurches forward, Gekko hops out then jumps onto a lamppost. He figures it will be safer OUTSIDE the Cat-Car! Wrong decision!

Romeo watches Gekko from inside his Lab.
"Which kind of clumsy will suit this sticky lizard?" he wonders, his fingers hovering over a flashing dial. "Fumble Fingers!" Gekko feels himself sliding off his post. What has happened to his famous Super Lizard Grip?

The PJ Masks begin to work out what's happening.
Romeo has invented a machine that can make
people clumsy!

ZAP! Lightning bolts of power strike everything in the
PJ Masks' path. Owlette finds herself caught in a ray.
"Now you're clumsy too, bird brain," cackles Romeo,
zooming off towards the park.
"You'll never fly in a straight line again."

"What are we going to do?" cries Gekko. "We'll be slipping and stumbling forever!"

Catboy has no doubts. "We're still the PJ Masks. It's time to be a hero!"

Back in the Cat-Car, Catboy tries to press the button for furballs to defeat Romeo, but he is still clumsy and presses all the wrong buttons. The Cat-Car drives off, out-of-control, and Catboy has to leap to safety as his super vehicle heads towards the Lab.

Romeo tries to steer the Lab out of the way. In his panic, he pushes the button to re-start the Clumsy Ray. "Nooooo!"
It is a big mistake. The machine zaps in all directions, reflecting its rays back towards the Lab!
"I've been zapped by my own rays," groans Romeo.

The PJ Masks head towards the Lab. This is their big chance to destroy the Clumsy Ray . . . if only they weren't so clumsy.

Catboy has an idea. "We need to use our clumsiness," he decides.
"Like Clumsy Power!" agrees Gekko. "Cool Chameleons!"

Gekko reaches for a street light and spins around it, gathering speed.
Suddenly . . . **Whoaaa!** He slips off and flies through the air. Owlette grabs him, and, using all her new twisty-turny power, whooshes him towards Romeo's Lab.

As Gekko knocks the ray from the roof it explodes with a **WHOOSH!**
It sends coloured sparks flying back towards the PJ Masks.
Their clumsiness is cancelled out!

"You PJ Masks ruin everything!" yells Romeo.
"The PJ Masks save the day!" cheer Owlette, Gekko and Catboy.

At school the next day, Connor lifts up his model volcano.

Amaya and Greg look on nervously.

"It's not like I'm clumsified anymore. I've got it," he says.

Connor wobbles across the room . . . straight into someone!

"Okay!" he laughs. "Maybe I haven't!"

THE END

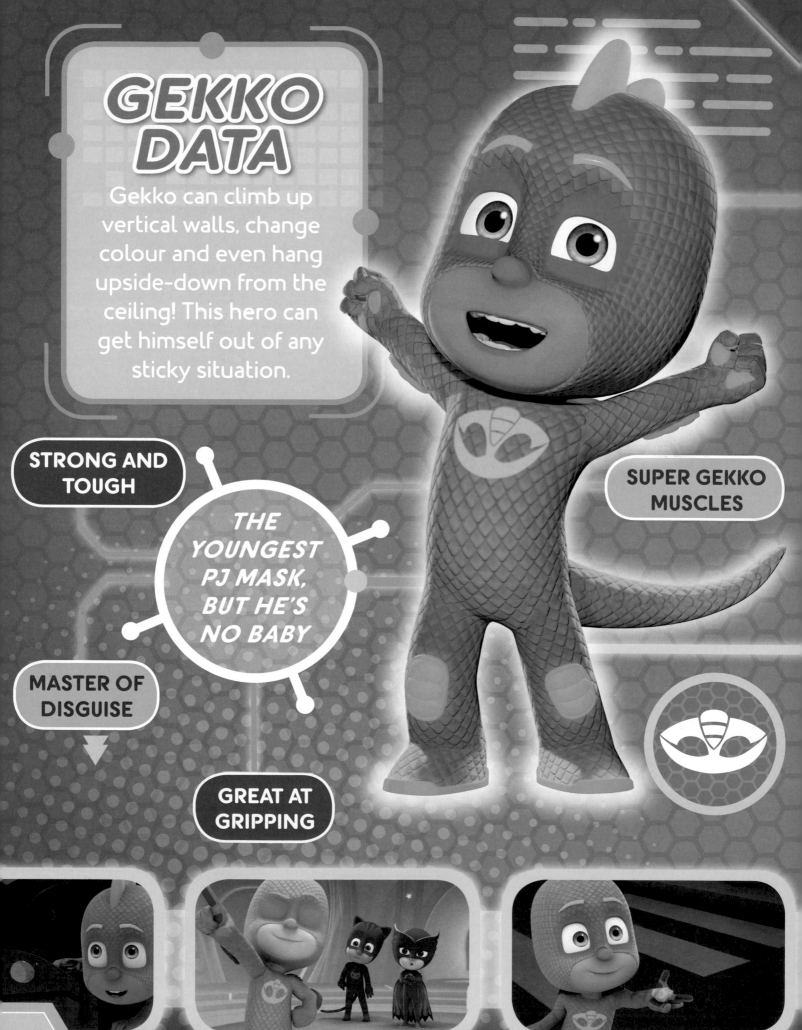

GEKKO DATA

Gekko can climb up vertical walls, change colour and even hang upside-down from the ceiling! This hero can get himself out of any sticky situation.

STRONG AND TOUGH

THE YOUNGEST PJ MASK, BUT HE'S NO BABY

SUPER GEKKO MUSCLES

MASTER OF DISGUISE

GREAT AT GRIPPING

TO THE GEKKO-MOBILE!

MULTI-TERRAIN VEHICLE

UPSIDE-DOWN? NO PROBLEM!

WATER JET

STICKS TO ANY SURFACE

GASPING GEKKOS!

SKILLS SLIDER

SPEED

SIGHT

HEARING

JUMPING AND LEAPING

MUSCLES

SKILLS IN THE SKY

SKILLS IN THE WATER

CAMOUFLAGE

BOOTCAMP TIME!

Gekko can bend himself into all sorts of shapes and get himself into all sorts of places! What would happen if you tried to turn yourself into a lizard, too?

What To Do:

Put both hands on the floor in front of you. Keep your knees off the ground.

Now move as quickly as you can across the floor. Ask a grown-up to watch your lizard skills!

Start by going forwards.

Then try moving backwards.

Now try scuttling sideways.

Wriggling Reptiles!

Got it sussed?

Try and keep one foot off the ground as you move. How does that feel?

Can you balance on just one hand and one foot?

What happens if you try to lift a hand instead?

COLOUR HUNT

Gekko's special suit can change to match any surrounding. This game is all about colour, and it is fun to play inside or out.

HOW TO PLAY:

1 Find a friend to play with. You will also need a timer and a grown-up to help.

2 When you're ready, each player should pick a PJ Masks character.

3 Set the timer to 60 seconds.

4 When it's time to start, rush around collecting up as many things as you can in the same colour as your chosen hero.

5 Ready, steady, run!

WILL OWLETTE TRIUMPH WITH A RED RECORD?

WILL CATBOY BE BLUE THROUGH AND THROUGH?

WILL GEKKO PROVE THAT HE'S KEEN ON GREEN?

Grab a bag for your things before you start!

When the time is up, count up who has collected the most objects. How quickly can you put them all back again?

31

MAKE YOUR OWN
STICKY SPLAT COOKIES

Ever wondered what a sticky splat tastes like? It's time to find out! Use Night Ninja's recipe to whip up your own batch of super-squidgy splat cookies. *MWA-HA-HA!*

INGREDIENTS

2 medium eggs

225g self-raising flour

100g butter, plus a little extra for greasing

1 tsp baking powder

75g caster sugar

1 tsp vanilla extract

1 tsp green food colouring

Makes 8 large cookies

3 Rub the ingredients together with your fingers, until the mix feels soft and crumbly.

Ovens are hot. Ask a grown-up to help you with this recipe.

6 Ask a grown-up to help you grease a baking tray with butter.

1 Ask a grown-up to pre-heat the oven to 200°C/400°F/Gas Mark 6. Wash your hands.

2 Crack the eggs into a little dish and give them a stir with a fork. Put the flour, butter and baking powder into a large mixing bowl.

If you want your splats to be a bit darker add a few more drops of colouring.

4 Tip the caster sugar and vanilla extract into the bowl, then add the eggs. Stir everything together with a spoon.

5 Carefully measure out the green food colouring and pour it into the bowl. Mix everything again until the dough becomes an even green colour.

Why not try using different food colouring to make cool splat cookies in lots of new colours?

7 Put your hand in the mixing bowl and tear off a lump of dough about the size of a golfball. Squeeze it into a lumpy splatty-shaped ball.

8 Put the ball onto the baking tray, then reach into the mixing bowl again and tear off another splat. Keep going until you have used up all of the mixture.

Bake your splat cookies for around 15 minutes, then put them on the side to cool. Super, splatty scrumptious!

LUNA GIRL DATA

If something catches Luna Girl's eye, she knows just how to get it. This villain's mighty moon power can drag anything into her grasp!

WATCH OUT FOR HER LUNA-MAGNET!

TERRIBLE TANTRUMS

MASKED BADDIE WITH MIGHTY MOON POWER

PEST OF THE SKIES

FOLLOWED BY A MASS OF MOTHS

LUNA BOARD

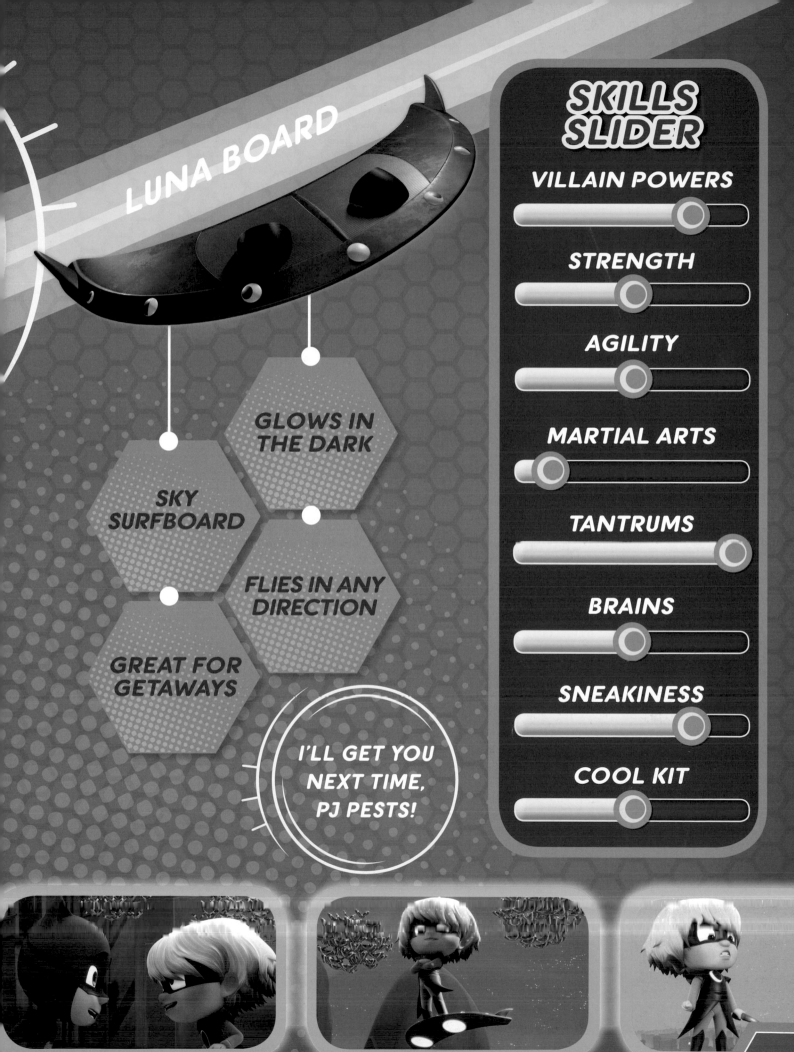

SKILLS SLIDER

VILLAIN POWERS

STRENGTH

AGILITY

MARTIAL ARTS

TANTRUMS

BRAINS

SNEAKINESS

COOL KIT

GLOWS IN
THE DARK

SKY
SURFBOARD

FLIES IN ANY
DIRECTION

GREAT FOR
GETAWAYS

I'LL GET YOU
NEXT TIME,
PJ PESTS!

Luna Girl's sneaky schemes keep the PJ Masks busy! Tonight she has been getting up to no good in the park. Use her test to sharpen up your spying skills.

Have a long look at the top picture.

★

Now cover it up. Five things are missing from the bottom picture. Can you work out what they are?

Three things have been added to the bottom picture. What are they?

LUNA GIRL ★ ★ ★

MAGIC MAGNETS

Luna Girl can use her Luna-Magnet to pull all kinds of things towards her. Imagine if your WHOLE body was a magnet! This game will show you how.

HOW TO PLAY:

1 Find a friend to be your partner.

2 Stand facing each other, then decide which one of you is going to be the magnet.

3 When the magnet moves an arm or leg, the other person must do the same thing.

If your friend raises their arm, you must raise yours, too!

4 Try making different shapes in the air, then see if your magnetic friend can make them, too!

5 Keep going until the magnet 'breaks' and one of you misses a move.

IMAGINE THAT THERE IS AN INVISIBLE THREAD BETWEEN YOU AND YOUR FRIEND, PULLING YOU WHEREVER THEY GO.

IF YOU ARE IN A BIG SPACE, THE 'MAGNET' COULD RUN, OR HOP, OR ROLL. THE OTHER PLAYER WOULD HAVE TO FOLLOW!

Moth Maze Mayhem

Luna Girl has been causing a LOT of mothy problems at the city school. Can you help the PJ Masks swoop in and save the day?

START

FINISH

Trace a path through the moth cloud all the way to the school gates.

Made it through the moths? Owlette is impressed! Colour in the hero's amulet.

IT'S TIME TO BE A HERO!

PJMASKS

PJ MASKS TO THE RESCUE!

MADE FOR MISCHIEF

Everything on this page is muddled up. Draw a line to match each object to its character.

The Ninjalinos can't stop making mischief! Now the little ninjas have stirred up more trouble for you to sort out.

Not even Romeo is safe! He needs to find THREE of his own things! Mwah ha ha!

SPEAK UP, GEKKO!

GREG IS NERVOUS. HE HAS TO READ A POEM OUT LOUD TO THE CLASS TOMORROW.

It's difficult. And embarrassing.

LATER, A STRANGE RED GLOW HOVERS AROUND HIM.

What's going on? My voice is getting quieter.

GREG HAS LOST HIS VOICE! IT'S TIME TO CALL THE PJ MASKS!

PJ MASKS, WE'RE ON OUR WAY. INTO THE NIGHT TO SAVE THE DAY!

Look, there's Romeo's Lab!

ROMEO HAS INVENTED A VOICE-STEALING MACHINE.

Hang on. If I don't have a voice, I can't read my poem!

Ha ha! PJ Pests! Now I have ALL of your voices!

ROMEO AIMS HIS MACHINE AT CATBOY AND OWLETTE, TOO!

THE VOICE-STEALING MACHINE CRASHES TO THE GROUND.

What's happening?

A BEAM HITS THE VILLAIN. ROMEO'S GADGET HAS SNATCHED HIS OWN VOICE!

No more voice stealing for you, Romeo!

THE NEXT DAY, GREG READS OUT HIS POEM.

Now I've got my voice back, this should be easy!

THE END

OWLETTE DATA

Owlette is always ready to rescue! She's a flying ace with enough hero skills to send any baddie running for cover.

POWERFUL EYESIGHT

FLIES LIKE A BIRD

SUPER-SMART MEMBER OF THE PJ MASKS

OWL WING WIND

OH SO ORGANISED

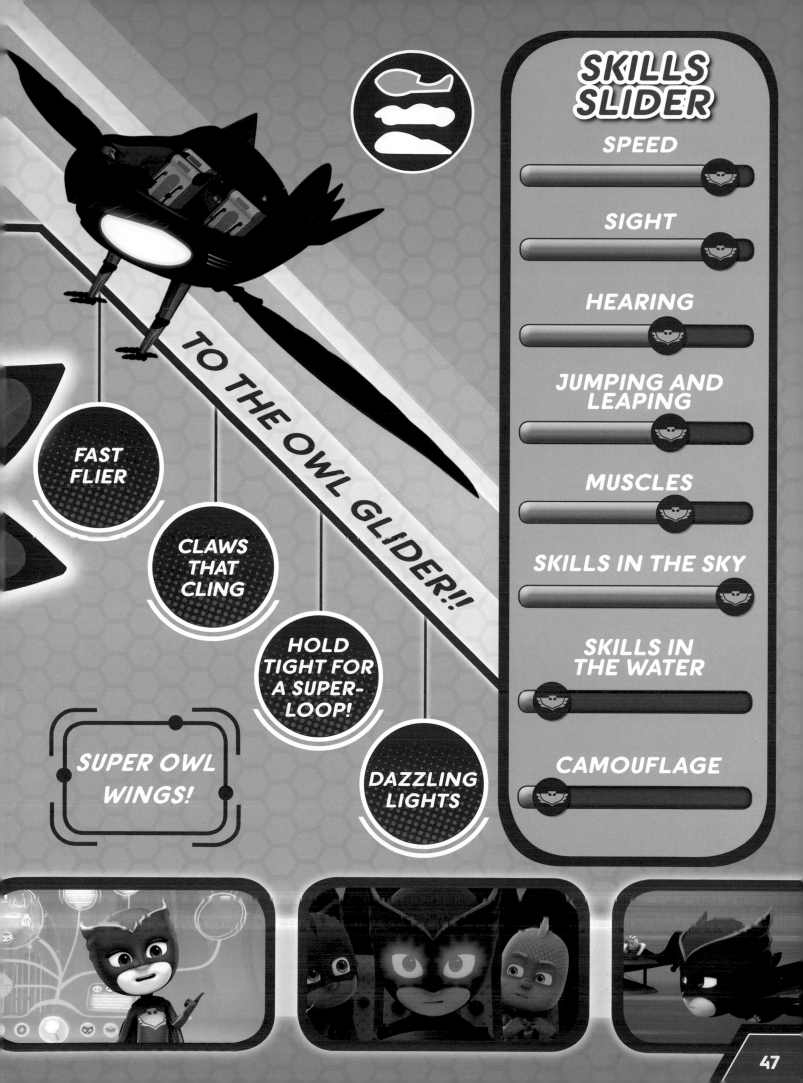

TO THE OWL GLIDER!!

SKILLS SLIDER

SPEED

SIGHT

HEARING

JUMPING AND LEAPING

MUSCLES

SKILLS IN THE SKY

SKILLS IN THE WATER

CAMOUFLAGE

FAST FLIER

CLAWS THAT CLING

HOLD TIGHT FOR A SUPER-LOOP!

SUPER OWL WINGS!

DAZZLING LIGHTS

★★ BOOTCAMP TIME! ▶▶

Owlette flies fast! Are you ready for a winged workout? Go outside, spread your arms and pretend to whoosh around like your hero.

Ask a grown-up to take you to the park.

Spread your arms out wide, take a deep breath, then . . .

Pretend to fly to the nearest tree and back.

Whoosh in a BIG circle five times.

Zigzag all the way to your grown-up at top speed.

You can play this with friends, too. Try to get faster each time!

OWL WING WIND!

★ ASK YOUR GROWN-UP TO SUGGEST SOME DIFFERENT PLACES FOR YOU TO PRETEND TO FLY.

★ TRY SPELLING OUT THE LETTERS OF YOUR NAME IN THE AIR AS YOU PRETEND TO FLY!

★ MAKE A SUPER SWOOSHING NOISE AS YOU GO.

48

OWLETTE ★ ★ ★

KEEP IT UP!

YOU WILL NEED:

★ A few light, plastic balls

★ Space outside to play

HOW TO PLAY:

When Owlette flies, no one can keep up! Have you got what it takes to soar like a bird? Play her game to find out!

1 Find a friend to play with you.

2 Choose a ball – make sure that you pick different colours.

3 Ask a grown-up to say 'Go!', then throw your ball up into the air.

4 Use your hands, body, legs and head to keep your ball off the ground.

5 How long can you keep the ball up?

The ball must stay in the air. If it touches the ground, the game is over.

6 The winner is the player who keeps their ball up the longest.

Want to make it super challenging?

★ Only use your feet to keep your ball up.

★ Touch the ball with a different part of your body each time!

49

CHAMBER DANGER

Night Ninja has trapped the PJ Masks inside the city museum! Can you rush to the rescue and help them escape?

EXIT

Did you manage to break out of the chamber? EXCELLENT WORK!

PICK AND MIX

Romeo has invented a cloning machine and filled the city with copies of himself! Help the PJ Masks pick out the real Romeo from the others below and put a stop to his badness.

TEST DRIVE

Which PJ vehicle would you most like to ride in? Take this tick test to find out! Answer the questions, then check the bottom of the page.

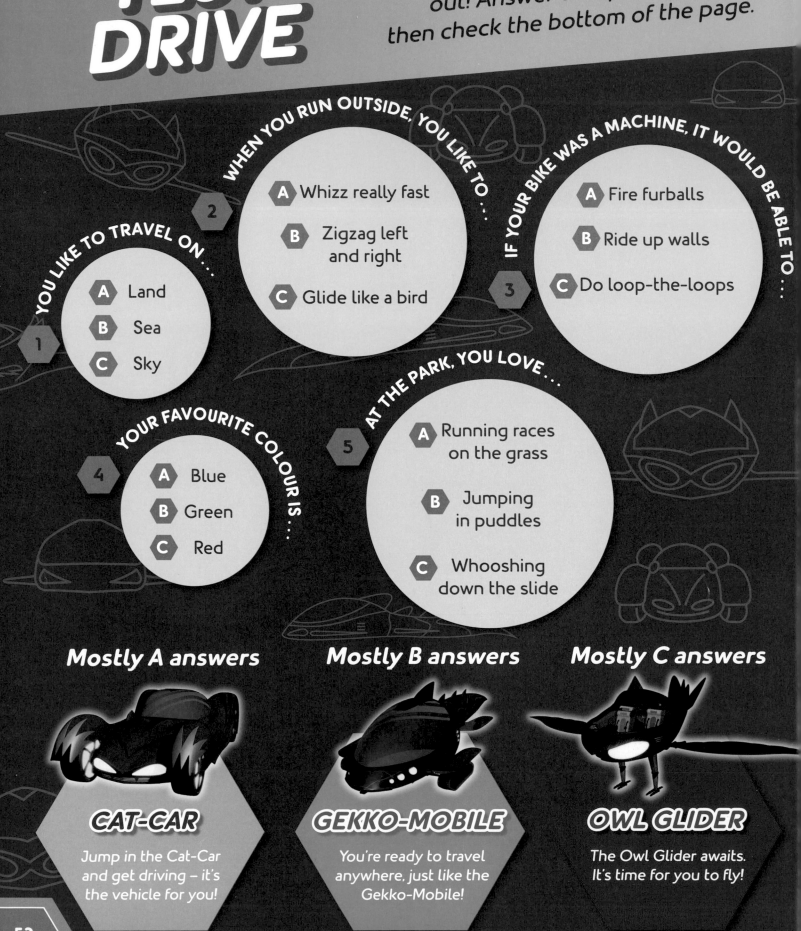

1 YOU LIKE TO TRAVEL ON...

- A Land
- B Sea
- C Sky

2 WHEN YOU RUN OUTSIDE, YOU LIKE TO...

- A Whizz really fast
- B Zigzag left and right
- C Glide like a bird

3 IF YOUR BIKE WAS A MACHINE, IT WOULD BE ABLE TO...

- A Fire furballs
- B Ride up walls
- C Do loop-the-loops

4 YOUR FAVOURITE COLOUR IS...

- A Blue
- B Green
- C Red

5 AT THE PARK, YOU LOVE...

- A Running races on the grass
- B Jumping in puddles
- C Whooshing down the slide

Mostly A answers

CAT-CAR

Jump in the Cat-Car and get driving – it's the vehicle for you!

Mostly B answers

GEKKO-MOBILE

You're ready to travel anywhere, just like the Gekko-Mobile!

Mostly C answers

OWL GLIDER

The Owl Glider awaits. It's time for you to fly!

FIRM FRIENDS

Owlette knows that the PJ Masks have always got her back. Now it's her turn – who is she swooping in to rescue tonight?

FIND A PENCIL, THEN JOIN UP THE DOTS.

1
2
25
16
3
17
24
23
18
22
10 11
4   9   20
19   21
15
5
8
6   7
12
14
13

ALL FINISHED?
NOW, DRAW IN AND
COLOUR SOME CITY
SKYSCRAPERS
IN THE BACKGROUND.

STAR-SPECKLED
NINJA SUIT

NIGHT NINJA DATA

Naughty Night Ninja wants to be the best at everything – splat sticking, karate kicking and stirring up trouble for the PJ Masks!

PESTER-POWER
TIMES A MILLION

SPEED, AGILITY . . .
AND BACKFLIPS

THROWS
STICKY SPLATS

MARTIAL
ARTS
EXPERT

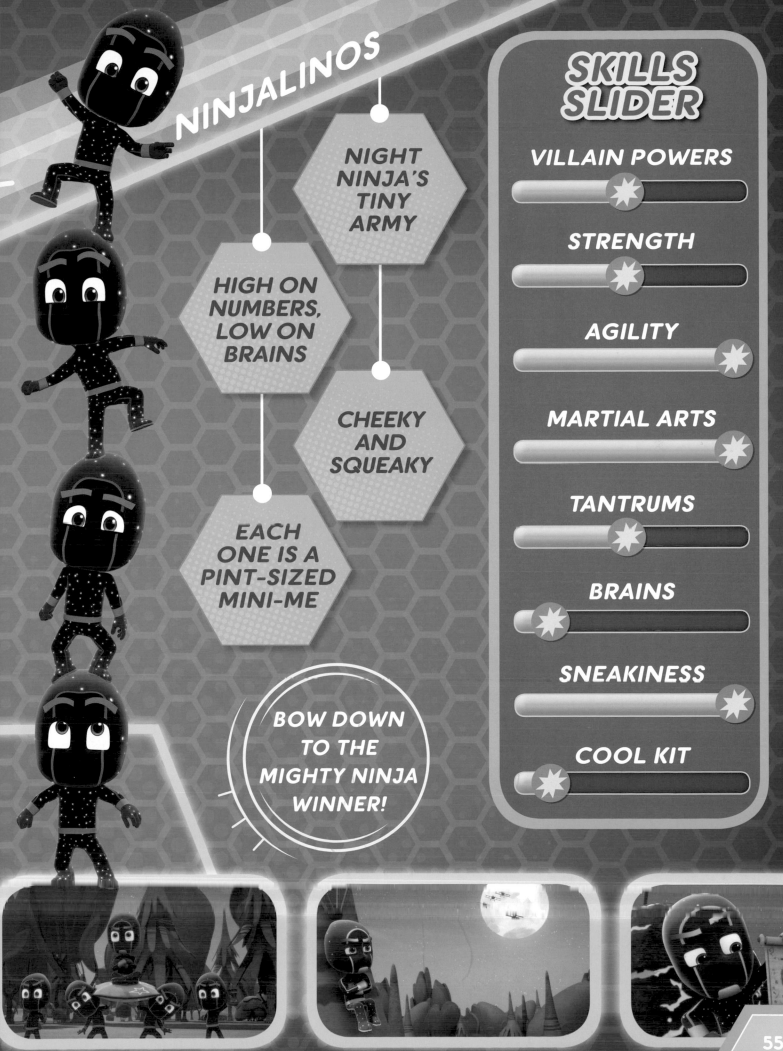

NINJALINOS

NIGHT NINJA'S TINY ARMY

HIGH ON NUMBERS, LOW ON BRAINS

CHEEKY AND SQUEAKY

EACH ONE IS A PINT-SIZED MINI-ME

BOW DOWN TO THE MIGHTY NINJA WINNER!

SKILLS SLIDER

VILLAIN POWERS

STRENGTH

AGILITY

MARTIAL ARTS

TANTRUMS

BRAINS

SNEAKINESS

COOL KIT

★★ BOOTCAMP TIME! ▶▶

Night Ninja can jump, hop and leap all over the place. Try his special workout to help you think like a Ninja, too.

What To Do:

Find a big empty space and stand at one end.

Now start to think like a ninja. How many ways can you get across that space?

★ WALKING. OF COURSE.

★ RUNNING. SURE.

★ HOPPING. OK.

★ SIDE-STEPPING. GOOD ONE.

★ BACKWARDS. GREAT IDEA!

★ ON YOUR KNEES, COOL!

If you try this with two people crossing TOGETHER there are even more ways for you to consider!

TRY AND THINK OF 10 MORE DIFFERENT WAYS TO TRAVEL.

DODGE, JUMP OR CATCH

HOW TO PLAY:

Night Ninja is a high-jumping nuisance, but if you keep practising, he might make you a Ninjalino! This is a game to play with a soft ball and a friend.

1 Stand a few metres apart from your friend.

2 Decide who will be 'Ninja One' and who will be 'Ninja Two'.

3 Ninja One must throw the ball towards Ninja Two. Ninja Two can try to dodge it, jump over it or catch it.

4 If the ball touches Ninja Two or they don't catch it, Ninja One gets a point and can throw again. If not, Ninja Two keeps the ball.

5 Keep playing until someone reaches ten points. This player is the Ninja Champ ... until you play again!

IF YOU PLAY THIS GAME WITH A FEW NINJAS IN A CIRCLE, IT GETS REALLY TRICKY! GIVE EACH PLAYER A NUMBER AND WORK YOUR WAY AROUND THE CIRCLE, TAKING IT IN TURNS.

PARTY PJS!

The moon is out, the sky is dark and the PJ Masks are having a concert in the park!

Look at this party picture, then join in with the fun.

1

WHAT MUSICAL INSTRUMENT IS OWLETTE PLAYING?

2

HOW MANY SWITCHED-ON SPOTLIGHTS CAN YOU COUNT?

DRAW A FUNNY FACE ON THIS PARTY BALLOON.

3

WHO IS STANDING IN THE MIDDLE OF THE STAGE?

4

WHO IS PEEPING OUT FROM BEHIND THE SPEAKERS?

5

WHAT COLOUR ARE THE CURTAINS?

ANSWERS

Pages 8–9
Night in the City

TRUCK HELICOPTER
COOKIE TROPHY
SKATEBOARD FOOTBALL
TREE CAKE
COMIC

THE PJ MASKS' HQ IS A
TOTEM POLE

Page 19
Crazy Crayons

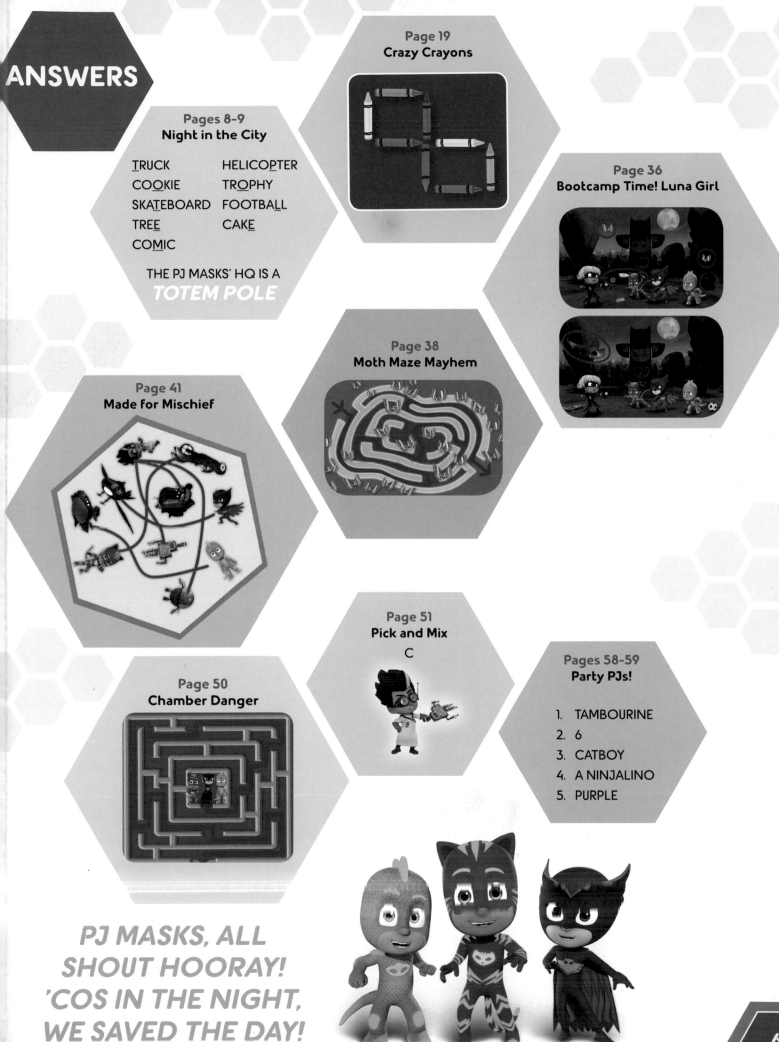

Page 36
Bootcamp Time! Luna Girl

Page 38
Moth Maze Mayhem

Page 41
Made for Mischief

Page 50
Chamber Danger

Page 51
Pick and Mix
C

Pages 58–59
Party PJs!

1. TAMBOURINE
2. 6
3. CATBOY
4. A NINJALINO
5. PURPLE

*PJ MASKS, ALL
SHOUT HOORAY!
'COS IN THE NIGHT,
WE SAVED THE DAY!*